Jasmine

The Missing Coin

This edition published by Parragon in 2011
Parragon
Queen Street House
4 Queen Street
Bath BA1 1HE, UK

ISBN 978-1-4454-4078-1
Printed in China

Jasmine

The Missing Coin

By Sarah Nathan
Illustrated by Studio IBOIX
and Andrea Cagol

PaRragon

Bath · New York · Singapore · Hong Kong · Cologne · Delhi
Melbourne · Amsterdam · Johannesburg · Auckland · Shenzhen

Chapter One

Princess Jasmine smiled as she gazed at Prince Aladdin. The royal couple was sitting on a tapestry in the palace garden, enjoying a warm sunny day. Aladdin was admiring his coin collection. He held up each gold coin, polished it with a cloth and then placed it carefully back in a wooden holder.

"How many coins do you have now?"

Jasmine asked, even though she already knew the answer. All Aladdin had talked about over the last few weeks was his coin collection.

"Twenty-three," Aladdin replied. "I don't have the complete desert collection yet. I need one more." He pointed to the empty

space on the wooden tray in front of him. "I have the snake, the scorpion and the cactus. All I need now is the camel."

Jasmine's father, the Sultan of Agrabah, had given Aladdin his first coin a few months before. Slowly, Aladdin had built up his collection. The desert coins were the most valuable – and the hardest to obtain.

"Maybe one will turn up soon," Jasmine said. She couldn't help but smile. For weeks she had been planning a royal birthday celebration for Aladdin. She knew that a camel coin was what Aladdin was wishing for, and more than anything she wanted to grant his birthday wish.

Jasmine patted Rajah's soft orange and white fur. The gentle tiger was lying near her, and he purred like a kitten as Jasmine stroked him.

Suddenly, Rajah's ears perked up and he sprang up from the ground.

"What is it?" Jasmine asked. "What do you hear, Rajah?"

Aladdin looked up and laughed. "Oh, Rajah," he said calmly. "That's just Abu back from the market." He pointed to the high stone walls surrounding the garden. "Hi, Abu!" he called. "Did you get those apples from Mr Kabali?"

Aladdin's monkey peered over the wall. He skillfully took hold of a low hanging branch and swung down to the ground. Even though Abu could have walked through the palace gates, he preferred to jump over the wall. A wide smile spread across his face. Eagerly, he hopped over to Aladdin.

"What?" Aladdin asked. "What is it?" He watched as the little monkey tried to act out what had happened to him.

Abu bounced around, making stepping motions. He pretended to bite into something and then prick his hand. He turned to face Aladdin and Jasmine and grinned proudly.

"You went to the market," Jasmine guessed.

Abu nodded his head, encouraging Jasmine to go on. After living with the monkey for a while now, Jasmine could tell what he was saying better than Aladdin could at times. "And you got apples and a

cactus?" She burst out laughing. "Why, that doesn't make any sense!"

Abu moved his head up and down so fast his small hat fell off! Then he reached into his vest and took out a coin. He held it out to Aladdin.

"For me?" Aladdin asked. He looked closely at the coin. Then he smiled at Jasmine. "Well, you got that right! Abu *did* get a cactus at the market. Look here," he said. He flipped the gold coin up in the air, and Jasmine caught it.

"Thanks, friend," he said to Abu. "But I already have the cactus coin. It's the camel I'm looking for."

Abu fell down in a heap on the grass. He was exhausted from his journey and from acting out his findings. He sighed heavily.

"It was a good try," Aladdin told him.

Jasmine flipped the coin back to Abu. "Sorry, Abu," she said. "You are sweet. Aladdin has been on the hunt for these desert coins for a long time."

"There aren't many of those camel coins," Aladdin said, shaking his head. "They are very rare." Aladdin was right – no one in Agrabah had the coin. This made him even more determined to get it, and Jasmine even more convinced that the coin would be the perfect birthday gift for him.

Jasmine walked over to Aladdin's collection. "But you have all the others." She put her hand on the coin rack. "Wait until Father sees what you've got here!"

"If only I had the camel coin," Aladdin said wistfully.

"Abu!" Jasmine called to the monkey, who was still sprawled out on the grass. "Are you ready for lunch?"

Abu sat up straight and nodded his head.

Jasmine knew that food had a way of cheering up the little monkey.

"Come," she said. "Let's go ring the bell for some food. I think it will be nice to eat outside today." She took Abu's hand, and they walked over to the palace.

Abu jumped up and pulled the long silk cord that was attached to the servant's bell. Inside, the palace chef would know that the royal couple was ready for some lunch.

"Abu," Jasmine whispered. She looked

over her shoulder and saw that Aladdin was far enough away not to hear her. "I just have to tell someone my great news!"

Abu scampered closer to Jasmine. He loved a good secret!

"You can't tell Aladdin," she said. "It's a special birthday surprise. Do you promise?"

The little monkey crossed his heart and motioned to zip his mouth closed. His eyes grew wide, and he nuzzled up to Jasmine.

The princess laughed. She checked one more time to make sure Aladdin wasn't listening. Then she turned to Abu. "I found the camel coin!" she exclaimed. "I just got word today. A messenger came all the way from Zagrabah! I'm going to go get it tomorrow." She reached out and gave Abu a tight squeeze. "Oh, Aladdin is going to be so surprised when his birthday wish is granted!"

Abu smiled at Jasmine. She looked so excited. But he had to wonder . . . how would the princess get all the way to Zagrabah and back before the royal celebration tomorrow night?

Chapter Two

After the royal lunch in the palace garden, Jasmine knew that she had to work on the second part of her birthday plan. In order to get the camel coin for tomorrow night's celebration, she would need some magic – specifically, a magic carpet!

How else could she get to Zagrabah and return before the party? Plus, she had to leave time to change her clothes and get her hair done for the big event. She was very excited about wearing her pink and blue dress with the beautiful jewels sewn onto it. She had had it made just for the birthday ball.

"That was a delicious meal," Aladdin said, leaning back against a tree. "My compliments to the palace chef. He is the best cook in all of Agrabah."

"Yes," Jasmine agreed. "He is good." She smiled coyly. "But remember the baklava from Zagrabah? It was out of this world!"

"Hmm, that *was* exceptionally good baklava," Aladdin said. His mouth watered as he thought about the sweet honey pastry with bits of nuts. "We should get some next time we fly there. Nothing beats having a magic carpet to take us where we want to go."

Jasmine moved closer to Aladdin. "Well, I was thinking that since tomorrow is your birthday, Rajah and I would go to Zagrabah and get you some."

Aladdin laughed. "Oh, I see," he said. "You want to take Magic Carpet? Have you ever driven it?" He raised one eyebrow and looked over at the princess. "It's a little trickier than you think. It doesn't just fly itself, you know."

"I know," Jasmine said. "I'm an excellent driver."

"Well, I should give you a quick lesson," Aladdin told her. "Just for safety."

Jasmine put up her hand. "Really, Aladdin, I'll be fine. Rajah will be with me. What could happen to me with him keeping guard?" She patted her tiger lovingly. "Besides, it's a quick flight to Zagrabah. We've been there hundreds of times."

Abu was sitting nearby, and he covered his ears. He didn't want to hear this discussion. He had made a promise to Jasmine not to say a word about the camel coin. The monkey was nervous that he might slip up and give away the secret! Abu reached over and took a banana from the large fruit bowl in the middle of the blanket. If he was eating, he couldn't make any noise!

Suddenly, Aladdin whistled sharply. The Magic Carpet came speeding towards them.

"Magic Carpet," Aladdin said, "I'd like you to take Jasmine and Rajah where they want to go tomorrow morning."

The Carpet stood up and shook its tassels enthusiastically. Then it zoomed over to Jasmine and nuzzled up to her affectionately.

Jasmine laughed. "See, we're good friends," she told Aladdin. "We'll leave early tomorrow morning. After all, we need to be back in time for the big celebration."

"You bet," Aladdin said, grinning. "Should be a great party. Genie said that he'd come by, too. You never know what kind of mischief he'll be up to!"

"You are right about that," Jasmine said. She reached out and gave Aladdin a hug. "I have a feeling it's going to be a birthday full of surprises!" Then she walked towards the palace to start preparing for the big journey.

Early the next morning, Jasmine and Rajah were ready to depart for their trip. Jasmine slung her bag over her shoulder. Inside the bag was a scroll with directions to the collector in Zagrabah. Jasmine was excited. This was going to be the best birthday gift ever!

She took a deep breath and then whistled for the Magic Carpet. It came speeding up to the palace balcony.

Rajah eyed the carpet with concern.

"It's okay, boy," Jasmine said. "We're going to have a fun adventure."

The Magic Carpet folded itself up to make steps so the princess and Rajah could climb aboard. It stood very still as its guests got on.

Aladdin appeared on the balcony just as Jasmine and Rajah were sitting down on the Carpet. Rubbing his eyes, Aladdin tried to block the bright morning sun. "Remember to look both ways before turning," he instructed.

"I know," Jasmine said, smiling.

All afternoon the day before, Aladdin had been full of advice on how to drive the Carpet.

"And always check to make sure that all hands, feet and paws are safely on the Carpet," the sleepy prince added.

"Of course," Jasmine replied. "We'll be fine and back before the party. Happy birthday!"

Suddenly, Abu came racing out of the palace. He was jumping up and down. Aladdin looked over at him.

"Abu says to be careful!" Aladdin called as the Magic Carpet started to slowly fly away.

The monkey jumped up and down again.

"And not to forget that he loves baklava,

too!" Aladdin said, laughing.

Jasmine smiled back at Aladdin and Abu. "Yes, I know," she said.

"One more thing!" Aladdin shouted. He waited until Jasmine had turned around. "Have fun!"

"We will," Jasmine said. "To Zagrabah!" she commanded the Carpet.

Magic Carpet lifted higher off the ground. With her long, dark hair flowing behind her, Jasmine waved good-bye. Suddenly, the Carpet dipped low and went zooming down to the palace garden.

Rajah let out a howl, and Jasmine pulled on the tassels gently to slow the Carpet.

"We're okay!" Jasmine called as they rose back up to the balcony. She saw the worried expressions on Abu's and Aladdin's faces. "Don't worry. See you later!"

Aladdin ran his hand through his hair and looked over at Abu. The monkey shook his head. New drivers made him nervous.

Jasmine looked back at Aladdin as she flew off. She sure hoped this ride would be smooth sailing!

Chapter Three

A few minutes later, a smile spread across Jasmine's face. The view from the Magic Carpet was magnificent. High above the treetops, she and Rajah had a glorious bird's-eye view. The beautiful palace looked even grander from the sky. Jasmine turned to Rajah, but when she saw the tiger's face, her smile disappeared.

It was rare that Jasmine saw fear in the

brave animal's eyes. She reached out to him and stroked his head. "You aren't used to being up here like a bird, huh?" she said. "There's no reason to be afraid."

Rajah raised one of his bushy eyebrows and growled softly. He much preferred his four paws on the ground at all times.

"Don't worry, Rajah," she said. "We'll be in Zagrabah soon enough."

She waved her arm and pointed to the sights below them. "Enjoy the view! See how small the tents in the marketplace look from up here?

"I don't know why Aladdin and Abu were so concerned," Jasmine huffed. "Look at us – we're doing just fine." She flipped her long hair to the side and settled back down on the Carpet. Peering over the tassels, she sighed. "This is the best way to travel. There is no other way we could have gotten to Zagrabah and back before Aladdin's party tonight. Thank you, Carpet!" Turning back to see Rajah, she started to chuckle. Her tiger had his paw over his eyes. "Don't worry," Jasmine told the scared animal. "I see the desert ahead. That means Zagrabah isn't too far off."

As the Carpet sailed through the clouds, Jasmine thought about how happy Aladdin would be when he saw his birthday present. He had no idea his wish was about to be granted!

The sands of the great desert came

into view, and Jasmine grew more excited. The party that evening would have all of Aladdin's favourite foods and friends. Genie would be there, along with many of the people from the marketplace. It would be a royal celebration fit for a prince. And the best part for Jasmine would be the look of disbelief on Aladdin's face when he saw the camel coin!

The dry desert air greeted them as the Carpet flew quickly over the sand dunes. Just as Jasmine was about to turn off to the left, the Carpet suddenly started shaking.

"What's going on?" Jasmine wondered aloud.

Rajah peeled his paw off his eyes to check on what was happening. He didn't like the concerned expression on Jasmine's face. Or the bumpy ride.

Jasmine held on to the tassels as the Carpet coughed and sputtered. Leaning closer to the Carpet she asked, "Are you okay?"

There was no reply.

And then the Carpet zoomed straight down.

Down, down, down into the desert dunes!

In seconds, Jasmine and Rajah found themselves covered in sand. Slowly, Jasmine picked herself up.

"Thank goodness that sand is soft!" she said, dusting herself off. She was relieved that she and Rajah were fine. But the Magic Carpet didn't look so good. It had rolled itself up into a tight scroll! "Oh, dear," the princess whispered.

She tried to roll out the Magic Carpet onto the sand, but the stubborn rug would not budge. "Something must be very wrong. I've never seen Magic Carpet behave like this."

Jasmine looked around. Maybe there is *someone* else out here, she thought. But instead of a person, a bright purple and green snake suddenly popped its head up from a sand dune near Rajah's paw. Rajah jumped straight into Jasmine's arms. The snake hissed at the princess and her tiger and began raising itself up into the air until it was as tall as Jasmine herself. The princess gasped.

Then the snake stuck out its tongue.

"Oh, Rajah," Jasmine said, relieved. "This snake isn't going to harm us." She smiled sweetly at the slithering animal. "Are you, Mister Snake?"

The snake seemed to give a small smile. Then he dove back into the sand. Rajah leaped out of Jasmine's arms. He shook out his fur and motioned for Jasmine to get on his back.

As Jasmine was about to climb up on her tiger, she looked down at her foot. "Oh, dear!" she cried. "It's a scorpion!"

Jasmine wasn't so frightened of snakes, but she knew scorpions could be especially dangerous. The scorpion snapped its pincers at Jasmine.

Then Rajah roared loudly and the small scorpion scampered away.

"Thank you, Rajah! I forgot that the desert could be a bit dangerous at times. But I don't think we're that far off from Zagrabah," Jasmine told him. "We can still get to the market for the coin."

Rajah roared and nudged the Carpet.

"And yes, let's hope that we can find someone who might be able to fix Magic Carpet!" Jasmine added.

Together they set off towards the west. Jasmine was on Rajah's back with the Carpet in her arms.

Far off, Jasmine could see the tall tents of Zagrabah. She hugged the rolled-up Magic Carpet, wondering what had happened to make their flight end so unexpectedly. She hoped that she hadn't done anything wrong. Suddenly, Rajah yelped. He sat down and started to lick his paw.

Jasmine quickly jumped off his back and examined the wounded foot. "Oh, dear," she cried. "There are cactus spines in your paw!

You must have stepped on a cactus."

Jasmine sat down on the hot sand. "A snake, a scorpion and now a cactus?" she said. "This is just like Aladdin's coin collection!" She hugged Rajah tightly. "But what we really need is to find a camel!"

Chapter Four

Rajah whimpered as he looked at his sore paw. Behind him, Jasmine spotted the prickly plant that he had stepped on.

"I'll be able to get those stubborn spines out," Jasmine said in a comforting tone. "It's not so bad." From her bag, she pulled out a cloth and a needle. "Good thing I brought my sewing kit with me," she mused.

Rajah's eyes grew wider. A needle was

for Jasmine's sewing – not his paw!

Turning, Rajah folded his paw underneath his body.

"Come now, Rajah," the princess coaxed him. "Your paw will feel much better once we get those pesky spines out."

The large tiger didn't move.

Jasmine gave him a loving hug around his thick neck and then reached for his paw. "Really, this won't hurt a bit. I promise that when we get to the market, we'll find you a special treat for being so brave."

The thought of food from the market relaxed Rajah, and he willingly stuck out his paw. He loved all the scents of the market. There were fresh fruits, roasted meats and the smells of other delicious foods. He licked his dry lips. Maybe there would be some cold water there, too.

"All done!" Jasmine exclaimed proudly. "I told you that wouldn't be so bad."

Rajah looked at his paw. No more cactus spines! He rubbed his head against Jasmine's hand happily.

Jasmine giggled as Rajah's fur tickled her. "Okay, we have to keep moving," she said. "I see the tents of the city, so we can't be far."

Lifting up his large nose, Rajah sniffed the air. There were some distant scents coming from the direction in which Jasmine was pointing. Rajah hoped they reached those scents soon!

Jasmine climbed on Rajah's back and the

pair set off again. But being in the hot desert heat was not easy. The sun was beating down on the two travellers, and they were both thirsty and tired.

"Oh, Rajah," Jasmine sighed. "This was not part of the plan! We don't have time to be wandering in the desert."

The large tiger shook his head. He wanted to lie down. He was exhausted.

"Look!" Jasmine cried. "I see water! And trees!" She pointed straight ahead. "And, my goodness," she gasped. "There is a family of camels!"

The happy sight made Rajah very excited. He gathered his last bit of energy and broke into a run. Camels meant a ride to the market – if they were lucky.

The three camels surrounding the oasis looked up at the two strangers quickly approaching them. It was not every day that a princess and a tiger came bounding through the desert!

Jasmine had spent time around camels before. Her father had a few in the menagerie at the palace. She knew that the animals were very cautious.

Slowly, the gentle princess approached the camels. She extended her hand in a friendly gesture. The largest camel stepped forward and sniffed her hand. The camel's nose brushed against her palm.

"Hello," Jasmine said. She smiled, trying not to let her nervousness show, as she watched the camel survey her. He had beautiful long eyelashes!

The camel took a step back when he looked over at Rajah.

"I am Princess Jasmine," she said. "And this is my friend Rajah. We are not here to harm you. We actually need your help."

The two other camels inched closer to Jasmine. The littlest camel came right up to her.

Jasmine giggled as the baby licked her hand. "Thank you," she said. "It's lovely to meet you, too."

The mother camel nuzzled her baby, and the baby stepped back.

"You see," Jasmine explained to the camel family, "we were flying on this Magic Carpet." She pointed to the rolled-up rug in her hand. Then she told the whole story of Prince Aladdin's birthday and his coin collection. "And so we need to get to Zagrabah to get the coin and have the Magic Carpet fixed. We have to make it back to the palace in Agrabah before the party starts." Jasmine paused. "Would you please help us?" she asked.

The camels exchanged a look. Jasmine held her breath. There was no way that she and Rajah could walk all the way to the market in time. They still had to find the coin seller in the market, and then find someone to fix the Magic Carpet. Jasmine sat down in the sand. How were they going to get back in time for Aladdin's party? Had she completely ruined his birthday?

The baby camel nudged Jasmine and nodded towards the water.

Jasmine looked up, tears in her eyes. "Thank you," she said. "Yes, some water would be nice." She cupped her hands in the water and took a few sips. It was cool and wonderful. Then she held out her hands for Rajah. He happily lapped up the water. When she turned back to the camels, the largest one was kneeling down, ready for a passenger.

"You'll take us?" Jasmine asked. "Oh, thank you!" She rushed towards the animal. "Thank you! Thank you!" she cried as she climbed up and sat between the camel's two humps.

The mother knelt down and Rajah leaped up on her back. The tiger looked a little uncomfortable, but he was happy for the ride.

"To Zagrabah!" Jasmine commanded. She was excited – and relieved.

Now she just hoped that they'd be able to find the coin and someone to help fix the Magic Carpet. As the camels strutted across the hot sand, Jasmine hugged the Carpet tightly. She sure could use a little magic now, she thought.

Chapter Five

"Zagrabah!" Jasmine exclaimed. Riding on the tall camel, she saw the tents of the market appear before her. "Rajah, we made it!" she said, turning around. Rajah was sitting up on the mother camel.

Jasmine laughed when she saw her tiger on the camel's back. His nose was high in the air as he sniffed the market's smells. "Don't worry, I remember my promise," she told him. "We'll find you a special treat for being so brave when I took out those cactus spines."

Rajah purred and hopped off the camel's back. He was ready to explore all those delicious smells – and get his treat!

"Thank you very much," Jasmine said to her camel. The camel stopped walking and knelt down low to the ground. The princess climbed off the animal and gave him a hug. "You were so kind to take us here."

The three camels all bowed their heads and turned to wander back to their oasis.

"We were lucky to find those friends," Jasmine said as she watched the camels head over the sandy hills of the desert. She looked down at the Magic Carpet still rolled up in her hands. "I hope we can find someone here to help the Carpet."

Together, the princess and the tiger entered the maze of tents.

"Come, let's find Zuhdi the coin trader," Jasmine said.

The market was bustling with people. There were more vendors here than in Agrabah's market. People were eagerly shouting at the beautiful stranger and her tiger. They wanted them to come over to their tents and buy something. Jasmine purchased some baklava and stored the package in her bag. But she kept moving. She wanted to get to Zuhdi's tent at the far end of the market.

Rajah was having a harder time staying

focussed. He smelled freshly baked breads and spotted ripe fruits and vegetables. There were so many delicious things! He wasn't sure which way to turn. And then his nose was tickled with a scent that made his stomach rumble. A smoky odour that could mean only one thing – meat being cooked!

"Zuhdi wrote that his tent was all the way in the back," Jasmine said, looking at the letter in her hand. But when she turned around, Rajah wasn't behind her!

She spun in a full circle, jumping to see above the crowd. How could she lose a large tiger?

"Rajah!" Jasmine called.

The tiger was nowhere in sight. Jasmine's heart started to beat very fast. First the Magic

Carpet had failed, and now she had lost Rajah? Maybe this day was cursed! She knew Rajah was a sweet, gentle tiger, but the other people in the market did not. She had to find Rajah before anything happened.

Jasmine started walking down one of the aisles of the market. All around her were people selling delicious-looking food, colourful rugs, shimmering jewels and beautiful clothing – but all Jasmine could think about was finding Rajah.

Suddenly, a man popped up in front of the princess.

"How about a sweet apple to cheer you up?" the man asked. He leaned over and showed Jasmine a shiny red apple.

Seeing the apple reminded Jasmine

of when she met Aladdin in the Agrabah market. She had learned a lot about markets since that time. The first lesson was that nothing was free! If she wanted that apple, she'd have to pay for it. And she didn't have enough money to buy everything – plus, she *had* to find Rajah!

"No, thank you," she said anxiously. "Did you happen to see a tiger roaming by here?"

The apple vendor raised his eyebrows. He clearly thought she was crazy.

"Ah, never mind," Jasmine added quickly as she hurried off. Then she smelled the smoky scent of meat roasting. Suddenly, Jasmine knew exactly where she would find her hungry tiger.

Following the smell, she made her way to the large fire pit on the far side of the market. There she spotted Rajah! She raced up to him.

"Oh, Rajah! I was so concerned!" she cried. "Don't ever walk away from me in a crowded market," she scolded him. But she couldn't stay mad when she saw Rajah's big green eyes. The poor thing hadn't meant to worry her!

Jasmine reached into her bag and took out some coins to pay the cook for the meat. Rajah was thrilled to have a large bone to carry through the market. He kept close by Jasmine's side as they walked to Zuhdi's tent.

When they arrived, Jasmine surveyed the tent. It was much smaller than all the others, and it didn't have brightly coloured silk flags hanging from it. She wondered if it was the right tent. Just then, an elderly man came out from the back.

"Hello, I am Zuhdi," he introduced himself. "How can I help you?"

"Hello, I am Princess Jasmine," Jasmine said. "I wrote to you about the camel coin. . . ."

"Yes, of course!" Zuhdi exclaimed. "You've had a long journey, Princess. Please come in and have some tea."

"Thank you, but we are in a bit of a hurry," Jasmine said as she followed Zuhdi inside. "It is my husband's birthday today, and we need to get back to the palace for the celebration."

The man scurried over to the back of the tent and disappeared behind a dark curtain. "I'll be one minute!" he called.

Jasmine played with one of the tassels on the Magic Carpet. "Oh, I hope he has the coin!" she whispered.

Zuhdi appeared with a long wooden box. "Here we are," he said. Jasmine held her breath as he lifted up the top to reveal a gold coin. It had a camel on it!

"This is it!" Jasmine exclaimed. "Oh, thank goodness you really did have the coin. That's about the only thing that has gone right today." She carefully took the coin out of the box and inspected the design. Aladdin was going to love it. But having the perfect gift would mean nothing if she wasn't at his birthday party to give it to him. How was she ever going to make it back in time?

Chapter Six

*T*ears began to form in Jasmine's eyes. Zuhdi watched the beautiful, dark-haired princess. His forehead wrinkled with worry. "My dear princess," he said, "what is wrong? Is this not the coin you wanted, after all?"

Jasmine was exhausted and felt helpless. She sat down on a chair and told Zuhdi the whole story. She began with her father's gift to Aladdin and how the prince loved to collect coins. She told Zuhdi about Aladdin's search for the camel coin. Then she explained about the royal birthday celebration and her big surprise. She didn't think he would believe her about the Magic Carpet, but that was all part of her sad tale. The Carpet was the only hope for getting back to the palace in time.

When Jasmine had finished, Zuhdi got up from his seat. He went behind a curtain and returned holding a tray with a teapot and two cups. He poured Jasmine some tea. Then he gave Rajah a bowl of cool water.

"That is quite a story," he said. He took a sip of his tea and lowered himself into a chair next to Jasmine.

The princess gazed at the floor. "I'm

sorry," Jasmine said sadly. "I should not have wasted your time."

"But I think I can help you," Zuhdi told her.

Jasmine looked up at him. "You can?" she asked, surprised.

Zuhdi nodded his head. "Yes. I have a good friend named Rana. He knows all about magic carpets. In fact, he has one of his own!"

Jasmine's dark eyes sparkled. "Does he live far?" she asked eagerly. She put her teacup down and inched to the edge of her seat.

"Not at all," Zuhdi said. "He is here in the market. I'd be happy to take you to see him."

Suddenly, Jasmine felt hopeful once again. She squeezed the coin in her hand. Maybe Zuhdi's friend could help the Magic Carpet . . . and maybe, just maybe, she and Rajah could make it back for the royal celebration!

"Come," Zudhi said. He stood up and motioned for the princess and tiger to follow him. "Let's see if Rana knows what to do about your no-flying carpet."

Jasmine and Rajah trailed Zuhdi out of the tent. Men and women rushed back and forth. They were carrying baskets of food and other goods. Following Zudhi through the crowd was difficult. He weaved in and out of the people and tents. But Jasmine and Rajah stayed close behind.

Zudhi stopped at a small tent at the end of a row. "Let me see if Rana is in. Princess, you can wait here," he instructed.

There was a rock nearby, and Jasmine and Rajah sat down. Jasmine saw the sun slipping towards the western horizon. "Oh, Rajah," she sighed. "It is getting late. The walk in the desert took up too much time."

Rajah purred and rubbed his head against Jasmine's leg.

"I know," she told him. "I am hoping that Zuhdi's friend can help us." She glanced down at her bag and took out the gold camel coin. "I want to see Aladdin's face when he gets this. If we miss the party, it will ruin everything."

Suddenly, Zuhdi came rushing out of the tent. He was followed by a short plump man. "This is Princess Jasmine," Zuhdi said, introducing his friend to the princess.

Rana bowed before Jasmine. "It is my honour," he said. "How can I be of service to you?"

Jasmine stood up and held out the rolled-up Magic Carpet. "We were flying from Agrabah, and everything was perfect. Then, when we came to the desert, the Magic Carpet stopped working. We landed in the dunes. I'm not sure what to do to make the Carpet fly again." She looked at Rana. "We need to get back to the palace before nighttime. Can you help us, please?"

Rana stroked his chin thoughtfully as he

looked at the Carpet. He tried to unroll it, but the stubborn rug sprang back into its rolled-up position. "Hmm," he said. "This is worse than I thought."

"Oh," Jasmine said, concerned. She leaned against Rajah. This was not a good sign.

"You were over the desert when the Carpet started to sputter?" Rana asked. He bent down low to the ground and examined the rug.

"Yes," Jasmine told him. "We were almost halfway over the desert."

"And did you have a paddle?" Rana asked.

Jasmine shook her head. "A paddle?" she asked. "We've never used a paddle when flying on Magic Carpet." Paddles were for the water, not the sky!

Suddenly, Rana turned and rushed back into his tent. Jasmine looked after him in confusion. Where had he gone?

Chapter Seven

$\mathcal{B}$efore Jasmine had too much time to worry, Rana was back with a large, flat wooden paddle. Rajah raised one of his bushy eyebrows.

"What are you going to do with that?" Jasmine asked.

"You must paddle the Carpet," Rana said calmly. "*Especially* over the desert." He looked up at Jasmine. "Since you have never used a paddle, I'm sure the Carpet truly needs this. No wonder you crashed!"

Jasmine wasn't sure what to think. What was Rana talking about? The princess moved closer to him and stared at the wooden paddle in his hands. The dark wood was old and looked very smooth.

"Do all magic carpets need a paddle?" she asked Rana.

Rana nodded his head. "Yes, Princess," he replied. "You must swat at all carpets occasionally with a paddle." He held out his paddle for her to see. "This paddle has been in my family for many generations. And it has been used on several magic carpets."

Jasmine bent down and lowered her head to the Carpet. "I hope this won't hurt you," she whispered. She gently touched one of the tassels. "We want you to be yourself again."

"Oh, the carpets like this. In fact, it actually tickles them!" Rana told her. "And they don't enjoy all the sand that gets in their weaves."

Zuhdi knelt beside Jasmine. "That does make sense," he said. "Think about all the sand in the desert. I'm sure it's not good for the Carpet."

"If you look closely, you can see the tiny grains stuck in it," Rana said. He unrolled a little of the Carpet and pointed to the sand.

When Jasmine saw the sand stuck in the wool, she gasped. "Oh, I didn't know!"

she said. "I'm sorry." She looked at Rana. "Please, can you help Magic Carpet?"

Rana bowed his head. "Yes, it would be my pleasure." He gestured to the rock behind him. "Please, Princess, have a seat over there. This can get messy."

With Rajah and Zudhi by her side, Jasmine moved over to the rocks. Rana raised the paddle and swatted the Carpet. Jasmine heard a faint cough, and then a giggle. After a few more strokes, and a lot of chuckles from the Carpet, it unrolled itself.

"One more!" Rana shouted. He heaved the paddle high over his head and swatted the Carpet for the last time.

The Magic Carpet sprang up and zipped around in a circle above their heads. It

stretched out and shook its tassels. Then it did a few dips and glides before floating in front of Jasmine.

Clapping her hands, the princess leapt from her seat. She ran over and gave Rana a hug. "Thank you!" she cried. "Magic Carpet seems as good as new."

"I'll say!" Rana exclaimed.

"I promise to keep an eye on the sand getting in the Carpet," Jasmine said. "I never want to crash in the desert again!"

"I have a spare paddle in my tent," Rana told her. "Please, accept it as a gift."

Jasmine blushed. She shook her head. "Oh, I couldn't," she said.

But Rana ran into his tent and came back with a small golden paddle. "This little one is good for travelling," he said. "And it would be my honour to present it to you and the prince as a gift." He bowed and lifted the paddle up to Jasmine.

This time Jasmine bowed her head to Rana. "That is a lovely gift," she said, taking the small paddle. "And I will be sure to always travel with it!"

Rajah gave a happy roar as the Magic Carpet continued to fly gleefully about. After being in such a tight roll, the Carpet was ready to go!

Jasmine smiled at her two new friends, Rana and Zuhdi. Then she had a wonderful idea. "How about you give this gift to the prince of Agrabah yourself?" she asked.

Rana's mouth dropped open. "Go to the

palace of Agrabah?" He gasped. Then he turned with his eyes wide to his friend Zuhdi.

"Yes!" Jasmine replied. "You and Zuhdi *must* come with us back to the palace. You have been so helpful. I know that Aladdin and my father would love to meet you."

"Th-th-the Sultan?" Zuhdi stuttered. "He would like to meet us?"

Laughing, Jasmine took their hands. "Of course he would! And you will be my special guests at the birthday ball this evening. It is going to be a magnificent celebration."

Zuhdi and Rana were speechless. It wasn't every day that they were invited to a palace for a ball.

Jasmine looked up at the setting sun. "But we'll need to get going. Rana, do you have a carpet for yourself and Zuhdi?"

Rana whistled the same way Aladdin did when he wanted his magic carpet. In a flash, a brilliant green and yellow carpet appeared. It folded into three steps for the passengers.

Giggling, Jasmine urged the two men aboard. "Oh, I'm so glad that you are coming!" she said. "This will be a wonderful surprise for everyone."

She winked at Rajah and then gave a loud whistle, too. The Magic Carpet was by her side instantly. As she and Rajah climbed up, Jasmine turned to her new friends. Her eyes sparkled with mischief.

"Shall we make this a race?" she asked.

"It would be my honour!" Rana said. He had a grin on his face that stretched from ear

to ear. He had not raced his magic carpet in years. What a royal surprise!

Jasmine smiled. "Then you're on!" she cried. Now that her carpet was fixed and she was going to make it back to the palace with Aladdin's special birthday gift, she was too excited to have a leisurely journey home. And the Magic Carpet felt ready to fly. The sooner they got to the palace, the sooner the party could get started!

Jasmine turned around once more to her friends. "See you at the palace!" she called. And then she was off!

Chapter Eight

"*H*old on, Rajah!" Jasmine cried. She was having a grand time racing with the Magic Carpet. Now that she had Rana's paddle, she knew exactly what to do when flying over the desert. She had no worries as she sailed over the sandy dunes. Halfway through the desert, she gave the Carpet a few swats with her new paddle. The Carpet giggled as sand flew out.

"*Wheeee!*" Jasmine cried as the pair went soaring ahead of Rana and Zuhdi.

Jasmine couldn't wait to tell Aladdin and her father about her journey to Zagrabah. They would both be thrilled that she had got the camel coin, and happy to meet her new friends.

Soon the Carpet sailed over the tents of the Agrabah market. "We're almost there, Rajah!" Jasmine said excitedly. "I can see the top of the palace!" She pointed straight ahead.

But Rajah was enjoying this ride even less than the first one. He lowered his head. While Jasmine loved the adventure, he was ready to be home.

As the Carpet approached the palace,

Jasmine could see Abu, Aladdin and her father in the royal garden. Aladdin and the Sultan were huddled together by a bench. They were probably polishing the coins while they waited for her.

"Here we come!" Jasmine shouted. And like an experienced flyer she guided the Carpet down into the garden in a smooth, graceful landing. "Hello!" she called out.

Abu started to jump up and down eagerly. He pointed at Jasmine and then up to the sky.

Jasmine knew at once that Abu was pointing to the other magic carpet.

"It's okay, Abu," she said as she climbed off their carpet. "Those are our new friends from Zagrabah. Rajah and I challenged them to a magic-carpet race!"

"Looks like you won!" Aladdin said.

Just then, Rana landed his carpet next to Jasmine. "You are speedy, Princess Jasmine," he said. "It was a privilege to race with you. Thank you."

Zudhi had his hands over his eyes. "Are we on the ground yet?" he asked. He sat frozen on the carpet.

"Yes," Rana said, laughing. He put his hand on his friend's back. "You can open your eyes now."

Zudhi heaved a sigh of relief and peeled his fingers away from his eyes.

"Come meet my new friends!" Jasmine called to her father and Aladdin. She introduced everyone and then handed Rana the golden paddle she had used.

"We wanted to give you this for your birthday," Rana said to Aladdin, presenting the paddle to the prince.

Jasmine saw the confused look on Aladdin's face. She quickly told the story about the Magic Carpet coughing and sputtering over the desert, the kind camels and Rana's paddle. The only part she left out, of course, was the *real* reason for her journey.

"Oh, my," the Sultan said, shaking his head back and forth. "You've had quite an adventure!"

"I'll say!" Aladdin added. "And we learned an important lesson about taking care of the Magic Carpet. Did you at least get what you wanted from Zagrabah?"

Jasmine reached into her bag for the wooden box. "Happy birthday, Aladdin!"

As Aladdin lifted the top off the box, his eyes went wide. "Jasmine! How did you ever find this?" he cried. He couldn't believe that a golden camel coin lay before him!

The Sultan poked his head between them to get a look at the coin. "What a wonderful surprise, Jasmine!" he exclaimed. "Now the collection is complete."

Aladdin spun Jasmine around in a circle. She laughed as he lifted her off the ground. "I'm just so glad that I could grant your wish," she told him.

"Who's granting wishes without me?" a voice boomed. Genie appeared with a

sizzling smile on his face. "And where is this royal birthday party fit for a prince?"

Jasmine and Aladdin hugged their good friend.

"The party is set to begin soon," Jasmine explained. She turned to her new friends. "Please follow Abu inside and he will show you where you can change. I am so glad that you are here to celebrate with us."

"As are we!" Rana and Zuhdi said at the same time.

"Abu, wait!" Jasmine called. She reached into her bag and pulled out the package of baklava. "This is for you. Thank you for keeping my secret."

Abu clapped his hands and took the special treat. Then he removed his cap and waved for the two men to follow him inside the palace.

"How's tricks?" Genie asked Aladdin, giving him a gentle shove. He saw the Magic Carpet and gave Aladdin a wink. "Where have you been flying?"

Aladdin laughed. "You'll have to ask Jasmine," he said. "She's the one who just had a big adventure on the Magic Carpet."

"And I'll tell you all about it," Jasmine said to Genie. "But first I need to change into my new dress. I have a birthday ball to attend, you know!" She turned and ran into the palace.

Genie and Aladdin glanced at Rajah. The tiger wagged his head from side to side. He and the Carpet went to sit down in the shade of a tree. Both looked as if they needed a long nap.

"Guess I'll have to wait for the princess," Genie said, laughing. "I don't mind. Nothing I like better than a good old palace party for my pal Prince Ali!"

Soon people started to arrive for the grand event. Rana and Zuhdi entered the royal ballroom in new clothes, gifts from Jasmine. They were thrilled to be at the palace. And they were awestruck when they saw the beautiful princess in her sparkling jewelled outfit.

Jasmine smiled at her guests. "I am very happy that we could all be here," she said. "Enjoy, and have fun!" Then she turned to find Aladdin. He was also wearing new clothes and looked very handsome. "Happy birthday, Prince Aladdin," Jasmine said.

Aladdin grinned at the princess. "This is a fantastic party," he told her. "Thank you for planning this and for getting the camel

coin. You have made this birthday the best one ever."

Then Aladdin led Jasmine out onto the dance floor. Jasmine glanced over at her father and all their friends: Rajah, Abu, Genie, the Magic Carpet, Rana and Zuhdi. They were watching her, smiling. And on the mantel above them all was Aladdin's coin collection. Now every spot in the wooden case was filled with a shiny gold coin. It was a day Princess Jasmine and Prince Aladdin would never forget.

Don't miss the next enchanting Disney Princess chapter book!

Aurora
The
Perfect
Party

*B*eing a princess is a dream come true. But sometimes, Aurora misses the days she spent in the woodcutter's cottage with the three good fairies. The princess decides to throw them a surprise party. She'll gather their favourite items from the cottage, and invite their forest friends to the castle! Can the princess keep her perfect party plans a secret from the fairies before the big day?